When Mother Was Eleven-Foot-Four

A Christmas Memory

Jerry Camery-Hoggatt

Illustrated by Mark Elliott

Revell
Grand Rapids, Michigan

For Bill and Lauren Younger,
givers of extravagant gifts
agents of grace
Jerry Camery-Hoggatt

For two proprietors of patience and care,
Mom—Frances Crawford Elliott
and Cheryl Van Andel
Mark Elliott

Text © 2007 by Jerry Camery-Hoggatt
Illustrations © 2007 by Mark Elliott

This children's version is based on the book *When Mother Was Eleven-Foot-Four*, © 2001 by Jerry Camery-Hoggatt

Published by Fleming H. Revell
a division of Baker Publishing Group
P.O. Box 6287, Grand Rapids, MI 49516-6287
www.revellbooks.com

Printed in Singapore

Library of Congress Cataloging-in-Publication Data is on file at the Library of Congress, Washington, DC.

ISBN 10: 0-8007-1836-4
ISBN 978-0-8007-1836-7

This is the story of the
Christmas of 1963, which is
when I learned what it means
to be a giver of gifts. But this
isn't just my story. It's also my
mother's.

My mother's name was Josephine Mary Knowles Hoggatt, and sometimes she didn't make any sense to me. She used to say she could be really tall. Eleven feet four inches, which is as tall as a real giraffe or an elephant with its trunk stuck straight up in the air.

"I don't need to be tall all the time," Mother said. "But when I'm at my very best, I'm eleven-foot-four."

There were eight children in our house—me, my sister, our three brothers, and our three cousins. Our cousins lived with us because my uncle was away in the Navy and couldn't take care of them. If you lined us all up by height, Mother would stand right in the middle. Even though she was a grown-up, she was really short, just four-foot-eleven-inches tall. I know third graders who are taller than my mother. How could she be eleven-foot-four?

"What I *meant*," Mother would say, "is I am tall on the *inside*."

That didn't make any sense, either. How could you be tall on the inside and short on the outside? Where did you find room inside for the extra *tallness*?

I could understand Mother wishing she was tall on the outside—to reach for things from the high cupboard, or wash the tops of windows, and especially to decorate the Christmas tree.

You should have seen her Christmas tree. It was the best Christmas tree anyone ever saw. It was twelve feet tall.

So when Mother said she had to be eleven-foot-four to make Christmas happen, I thought she meant that she pretended to be tall in order to hang all of the ornaments. Only pretending didn't help. She still had to stand on a chair.

Every year she would wrap the tree in great big lights that glowed softly. Then she would tuck in tiny, twinkling lights. Next came long strands of popcorn strings. Then the store-bought ornaments she got from friends, and after that, all the handmade ones that we had brought home from Sunday school. There were paper plate angels with the faces of us eight children pasted on them. There were plaster-of-Paris handprints so heavy they pulled the tree branches to the floor. There were walnut halves with tiny statues of baby Jesus glued inside. My Sunday school teacher called each one "the gospel in a nutshell."

At the very top of Mother's Christmas tree perched a wonderful porcelain angel she had inherited from my grandmother. The angel was always the last decoration, and family tradition said it was supposed to be put in place by the youngest child in the family. This was a problem, because the youngest child, my cousin Pudge, was too short to reach the treetop, even when he stood on a chair.

My older brother John solved the problem with a brass ring, a paper clip, and a fishing pole. He sewed the brass ring to the back of the angel's dress. He tied the paper clip to the fishing line and hooked it to the ring. He used the fishing pole to lower the angel into place like a crane operator. When everything was ready, Pudge got to turn on the lights . . .

and all at once, like magic . . .

it was Christmas.

Underneath my mother's Christmas tree were lots of presents, more presents than I could count, and that had to be a lot because by the time I left kindergarten I could count to a hundred with my eyes closed. There had to be lots of presents because there were so many of us children: Joyce, John, Jim, me, Joel, and our cousins Nathan, Vickie, and Pudge.

I remember the day I discovered where the presents came from. Back in a corner of the living room was a little door. Behind that door was a tiny room Mother called the "Snake Room."

"Don't ever go in the Snake Room," Mother warned us.

"Why not?" I asked.

"It's full . . . of snakes."

"What do the snakes eat?" I asked.

"They eat each other," she said. "And spiders. And little boys."

I wasn't a little boy. I was eight years old. I had to see for myself. I went into the Snake Room.

It ruined Christmas for me that year. It turned out the Snake Room was where Mother hid her Christmas presents before she wrapped them.

It's lonely knowing that on Christmas morning you're going to have to pretend to be surprised, so I showed Joelie the presents too.

Who wants to pretend alone?

Every year then it was the same: Mother found a twelve-foot Christmas tree, covered it in lights and decorations, saw her porcelain angel placed on top, and made sure that underneath there were more presents than a person could count.

Not that counting mattered. When I was seven, I found out that Mother didn't count the presents either. She said you shouldn't keep track of how many presents you give or get, or measure the worth of a gift by how much it cost.

Mother, you see, was what grown-ups call a romantic. That meant she loved things grand and good and beautiful. She was extravagant too, which meant she never kept track of what a gift might cost. She said that Christmas was God's extravagant gift to us. Then she said, "If God gives extravagant gifts, why shouldn't we?"

Then one year, everything changed. My uncle left the Navy, got married, and took our cousins back to live with him. My older sister Joyce and brother John grew up all at once and moved away too.

Then our father left.

We went from being a big family to just Mother and three of her children: Jim, me, and Joelie.

Then Mother said we couldn't afford to live in such a large house anymore, so we moved away too.

For the first time there was no money for a Christmas tree, not any tree at all.

Mother went out behind the tiny little house where we had moved. Some old boards had been left in a pile. With a hammer she pulled out a bunch of nails.

Back in the house we helped her move aside the sofa. She took down the picture of Jesus from the wall and hammered the nails in the shape of a large triangle. She used more nails to tack up two or three strands of lights, some strings of popcorn, a few of the store-bought ornaments, and some of the handmade ornaments we made in Sunday school. She added one final nail above the point of the flat triangle Christmas tree, and there she hung her mother's porcelain angel, using the brass ring John had sewn on the back of the angel's gown. Mother gave the signal to Joelie. He turned the switch that made the lights come on.

Like magic, it was Christmas.

But it was different from all our other
Christmases. It was the first time I ever saw
my mother cry.

Was it because she missed the twelve-foot Christmas tree? Or because she knew that the only presents we would get that year were things we would have gotten anyway: underwear, socks, T-shirts?

I didn't know for sure.

I sat down beside her, and my tiny little mother put her head on my shoulder.

In all her life, she said, she had never felt so small.

My brothers and I made up our minds that this would never happen to our mother again.

We began to save our money.

We washed the neighbor's car for fifty cents. One time.

We put the fifty cents in a Mason jar that we hid behind the books on the shelf above Jim's bed.

We walked old ladies to their cars at the grocery store up the road. Sometimes they gave us a dime. Sometimes they pretended we weren't there. Then Mr. Cavender, the owner, chased us away with a meat cleaver. He had been cutting up meat to sell. We never went back after that.

We helped Mr. Flory put up the lights for the Christmas tree lot next to his peanut stand. He gave us each a quarter for that.

We collected soda pop bottles and turned them in for their California Redemption Value. In 1963, that was three cents each.

On the first Monday of December, my brother Jim counted up the money.

Four dollars and fifty-seven cents.

As soon as Mother left for the grocery store, we sneaked off to Mr. Flory's Christmas tree lot. He had saved a tree just for us. It was the only tree that could be had for four dollars and fifty-seven cents. We didn't care that this tree was shorter and more lop-sided than the trees Mother used to find—or that it had branches on only one side. We carried it home.

Then we moved the sofa. We took down the picture of Jesus. Jim tied a string to the top of the tree, and we hung it on the wall like a picture.

I began to hang a strand of those big Christmas tree lights that give off a soft glow, then another strand of smaller, twinkling lights. Joelie went in the kitchen and made popcorn strings to weave through the branches. Jim got out Mother's ornaments, and we hung some of the store-bought ones and some of the handmade ones. Jim put a nail in the wall above the top of the tree and hung our grandmother's porcelain angel by the brass ring on the back of her gown.

Then we went into the kitchen to wait.

It was dark when Mother came through the back door. She stepped into the house and hesitated a moment. She knew something was different in the house, but I don't know what gave it away.

Maybe it was the tiny bits of popcorn on the floor we had forgotten to sweep up.

Maybe it was that we were sitting in the dark. We were so excited we had forgotten to turn on the lights.

I think it was the smell of pine needles.

As Mother followed her nose down the hallway, we squirmed. Just as she turned the corner into the living room, Joelie turned on the lights.

All at once, like magic,
it was Christmas.

And it was the second time I saw my mother cry.

I thought at first that she cried because our little tree was nothing like the twelve-foot trees we had all those years.

Then I thought she must be crying because she was happy.

Or maybe because she knew all at once that we were going to be all right.

I'm still not sure. But I can tell you why I cried that day.

The three of us boys had looked across the room at Mother, and she stood up straighter.

Each of us straightened. We stood tall, taller than we'd ever been, tall as we could.

For the first time in our lives, we knew what it felt like to be taller than a real giraffe, or an elephant with its trunk stuck straight up.

We were our very best.

We were romantic.

We were extravagant.

We were, each of us, eleven-foot-four.

We were tall and wise, for that Christmas we
received what Mother wanted more than any pres-
ent she put under any tree.

We learned what it means to be a giver of gifts.